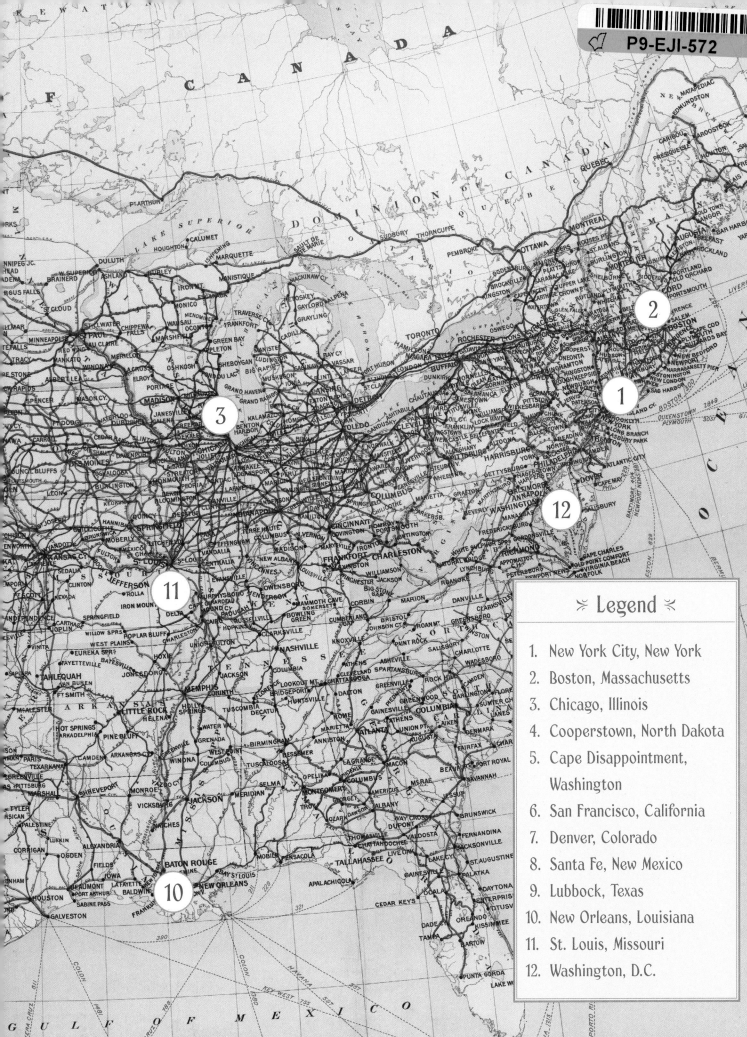

### ≈ Legend ≈

1. New York City, New York
2. Boston, Massachusetts
3. Chicago, Illinois
4. Cooperstown, North Dakota
5. Cape Disappointment, Washington
6. San Francisco, California
7. Denver, Colorado
8. Santa Fe, New Mexico
9. Lubbock, Texas
10. New Orleans, Louisiana
11. St. Louis, Missouri
12. Washington, D.C.

# Adèle & Simon
## IN AMERICA

Barbara
McClintock

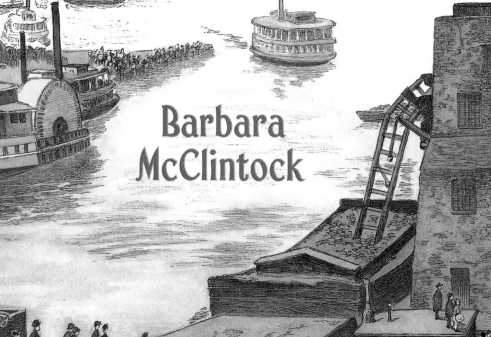

CUNARD

Frances Foster Books

Farrar, Straus and Giroux    New York

Adèle and Simon had traveled all the way from Paris to New York City to visit their Aunt Cécile. But that was just the beginning of their journey. Aunt Cécile was taking them on a train trip around America.

The night before their departure, Adèle, Simon, and Aunt Cécile were busy packing. Adèle spread Simon's things out on his bed. There was a journal, a pencil box, a cowboy hat, a tin drinking cup, a canteen, a bandanna, a pair of binoculars, a map, a pocketknife, a jacket, a vest, and a pair of bright red suspenders.

"*Please* try not to lose anything on our trip," sighed Adèle. "Don't worry, Adèle," said Simon as he hopped around the bed. "Well, I've labeled Simon's things with his name and my address," said Aunt Cécile. "Just in case."

The next morning, Adèle and Simon and Aunt Cécile arrived at the
train station. People were rushing to and fro, darting around
suitcases and trunks piled high on baggage carts. As Adèle, Simon,
and Aunt Cécile were about to board their train, Adèle stopped Simon.
"Weren't you carrying your journal?" she asked.
"Journal? What journal?" answered Simon.

Everyone looked up and down the platform. And looked. And looked.
But the journal was not to be found.
"We haven't even started our trip and you've already lost something!"
moaned Adèle.
Simon was up the steps and inside the train before she could scold him.

Their first stop was Boston. Adèle, Simon, and Aunt Cécile walked
all around the city and through the park. They took a boat ride on the
lagoon, gliding past tall willow trees and under a bridge. Adèle and
Simon were delighted. Aunt Cécile was happy to put her feet up.
Adèle wanted to sketch the boat. "Simon, could I borrow your pencil
box?" she asked.

But Simon was too busy watching a family of ducks to hear her.

"Where is your pencil box?" asked Adèle, louder this time.

Simon just shook his head.

"First you lost your journal, and now your pencil box is missing!"

Adèle frowned.

"That's okay," said Simon. "Let's feed the ducks next!"

From Boston, Adèle, Simon, and Aunt Cécile were on a train a day and a night, traveling past farms and little towns. When they got to Chicago, they walked along busy streets crowded with people and trolley cars. Bells rang, and horns and whistles blew. But Adèle and Simon were so fascinated by the sights that they barely noticed the noise.

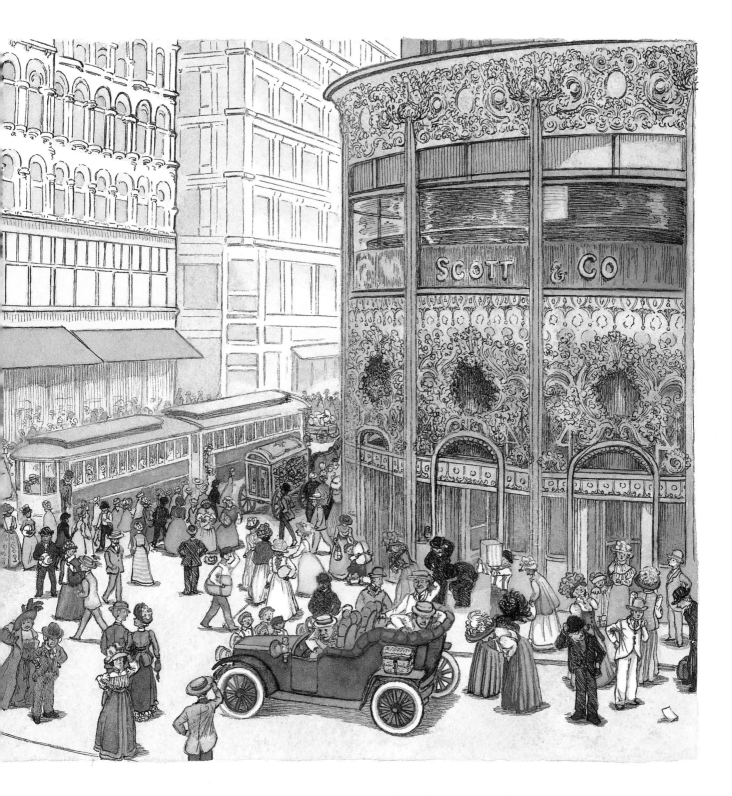

"Simon, weren't you wearing your cowboy hat?" asked Adèle.

"I was just a minute ago," said Simon.

They retraced their steps, scanning the sidewalks and street. The cowboy hat was gone.

"I don't believe this," grumbled Adèle.

Aunt Cécile had friends who lived on a farm in North Dakota.
Adèle and Simon fed chickens and patted cows and explored the barn.
The smell of freshly baked biscuits drew them back to the farmhouse.
Aunt Cécile met them with a pitcher of warm milk.

"Simon, where is your tin drinking cup?" asked Aunt Cécile.

"I don't know," said Simon. "I had it this morning."

Everyone hunted high and low for Simon's tin cup. Nobody found it.

"Simon, will you stop losing things!" said Adèle.

"Okay, Adèle." Simon smiled.

South of Seattle on the Pacific coast, Adèle, Simon, and Aunt
Cécile visited Cape Disappointment. But they were far from being
disappointed by the steep cliffs and strong, salty breeze, and the cool
waves rolling up onto the beach. They took off their shoes and
walked barefoot in the sand, past a family digging for clams.

"Just think, Simon—we're halfway around the world from our
home in Paris!" shouted Adèle.

"Adèle," Simon shouted back, "my canteen is gone!"

Simon was right. His canteen had disappeared without a trace.

"Don't worry!" Simon said. "I still have all my other things."

When they got to San Francisco, Aunt Cécile took Adèle and Simon
to Chinatown. They wandered up and down the narrow streets, ate
dim sum, and bought dried plums for dessert.
"Simon, weren't you wearing your bandanna today?" said Aunt Cécile.

"I thought I was. Maybe I took it off, just to be more comfortable,"
said Simon. "But I still have my binoculars and my map, my
pocketknife and jacket and vest, and, of course, my red suspenders."
"Oh, Simon! How can you lose your things like this?" scolded Adèle.

In Denver, Aunt Cécile hired a guide to take them up into the Rocky Mountains. After days of train travel, they were eager to be outdoors. They rode burros along winding trails near the edge of a steep gorge.

"I'm thirsty," said Simon.

"If you hadn't lost your canteen, you'd be fine!" grumbled Adèle.

"Simon, use your binoculars. I see a mountain goat!" said Aunt Cécile.

When Simon reached for his binoculars, he couldn't find them.
They looked everywhere, and looked again. After a while, they
gave up looking.

"Why can't you stop losing things?" sighed Adèle.

But Simon didn't hear her. He was chatting away with the guide
as they rode ahead on the trail.

When Adèle, Simon, and Aunt Cécile reached Santa Fe, they walked
around the plaza, passing families out for an afternoon stroll. The air
smelled of piñon fires and roasted chili peppers.

"Simon, may I look at your map to see where we are?" asked Adèle.

"I don't know where my map is," Simon said. "It must have fallen out
of my pocket."

"You've lost your journal, your pencil box, your cowboy hat and tin cup
and canteen and bandanna—even your binoculars. And now your map
is missing!" Adèle complained. "How can you keep losing things?"
"Don't worry, Adèle, we can always borrow Aunt Cécile's map," said
Simon. He looked up at Aunt Cécile and squeezed her hand.
Aunt Cécile smiled and squeezed back.

Adèle and Simon and Aunt Cécile visited a ranch in Texas. They rode
horses all day along a dusty trail and ate beans cooked on a campfire for
dinner. When the sun began to set, the cowpokes got out their pocketknives
and began to whittle pieces of wood as they sat around and talked.
"Adèle, do you know where my pocketknife is?" asked Simon.

Adèle and Simon and Aunt Cécile and all the cowpokes hunted high
and low. The pocketknife had vanished.

"Oh, well," shrugged Simon.

"You are hopeless," Adèle sighed.

New Orleans was alive with laughter and music, and the sounds of people speaking French. Adèle and Simon felt right at home. As they walked up and down the streets, Adèle noticed that Simon wasn't wearing his jacket.

"I don't know where it is," said Simon.

"I am really tired of looking for your journal and cowboy hat and canteen and binoculars and all of the other things you've lost along the way. And now your jacket is gone!" scolded Adèle.

"Don't worry!" said Simon. "It is too warm to wear a jacket anyway. I am much happier without it!"

In St. Louis, Adèle, Simon, and Aunt Cécile decided to take a ride on a steamboat. As they waited to board, they looked out over the wide Mississippi River, filled with boats of all shapes and sizes. The steamboats, with their huge paddlewheels and tall smokestacks, were the most impressive.

The sun was hot, but Simon didn't feel overly warm. That was because he wasn't wearing his vest.

"I had it on a minute ago," he said to Adèle and Aunt Cécile.
They looked all over, inside barrels and behind piles of rope.
The vest was nowhere to be found.
The steamboat whistle blew. It was time to board. Simon was the
first one up the gangplank.
"That Simon!" said Adèle as she and Aunt Cécile followed him
onto the deck.

Their last stop was Washington, D.C. Adèle, Simon, and Aunt Cécile
strolled along the Mall. Aunt Cécile showed them the Washington
Monument, the Smithsonian Institution, and the U.S. Capitol.
Out of the corner of her eye, Adèle noticed Simon tucking in his
shirttail. "Simon, your suspenders are missing!" said Adèle.
"I guess they are," said Simon.

They looked here, they looked there, they looked and looked and looked. "I can't believe this! You have lost everything. Your things are scattered all around America!" fumed Adèle.

But Simon wasn't thinking about his things. "Let's climb all the steps of the Capitol, Adèle! May we, Aunt Cécile?" Simon smiled.

Adèle and Simon were happy to get back to Aunt Cécile's apartment in New York City. The mailman had left a big pile of packages inside the front door.

"Goodness! These are all for Simon," said Aunt Cécile. "What could they be?"

Simon opened the packages, and there were his lost things—
his journal, pencil box, cowboy hat, tin cup, canteen, bandanna,
binoculars, map, pocketknife, jacket, vest, and red suspenders!—
sent from all the places they had visited.
"I knew we'd find them!" said Simon.

"Thank you for taking us all around America, Aunt Cécile," said Adèle.

"Can we take another trip?" asked Simon.

"Maybe someday, Simon, but first you two had better get a good night's sleep. Good night, Adèle. And good night, Simon."

"Good night, Aunt Cécile," said Adèle.

But Simon didn't say anything. He was already fast asleep.

The *Lusitania* was a British luxury ocean liner owned by the Cunard Steamship Line. Its maiden voyage was to New York Harbor in September 1907. On May 7, 1915, at the beginning of World War I, it was hit by a German torpedo and sank in 18 minutes. Most passengers on board perished.

Adèle and Simon are met on the dock in New York City by their Aunt Cécile. Among the crowd are the intrepid Tintin, Snowy, and Captain Haddock.

Aunt Cécile's apartment in New York City overlooked Washington Square Park—the backdrop for stories by Edith Wharton and Henry James.

Grand Central Station in New York City was undergoing great changes in 1908. An excavation project to build the underground rail system still used today was in progress. A new terminal was also being built, all without disrupting the close to six hundred trains a day that went in and out of the station.

Helping Simon look for his journal are Alfred Stieglitz, W.E.B. DuBois, Edith Wharton, Emma Goldman, J. P. Morgan, and engineer William J. Wilgus.

The Boston Public Garden was established in 1837. Located on what had been salt marshes near the edge of Boston Common, it is the first public botanical garden in the United States. The 24-acre garden is home to a nearly four-acre pond, swans, ducks, and the swan boats made famous by Robert McCloskey in *Make Way for Ducklings*, as well as what has been called the world's smallest suspension bridge.

The intersection of State and Madison streets in Chicago, Illinois, once called "the busiest corner in the world," is the location of the Carson, Pirie, Scott and Company Building, designed by Louis Sullivan. It is now a historic landmark and a famous example of early modern architecture.

Helping Simon find his cowboy hat are Theodore Dreiser, Sarah Bernhardt, Frank Lloyd Wright, Louis Sullivan, and Chicago Cubs players Joe Tinker, Johnny Evers, and Frank Chance, whose team won the 1908 World Series.

The Herigstad farm in Cooperstown, North Dakota, was originally homesteaded in 1881 by the author's Norwegian ancestors. The original sod house was replaced by a clapboard farmhouse and a barn and granary in 1903.

Cape Disappointment is located where the Columbia River flows into the Pacific Ocean in Ilwaco, Washington. It was here that Lewis and Clark reached the end of their long westward passage in 1805. For over two thousand years this area has been home to the Chinook Indians. Their population was devastated by diseases introduced by white people arriving as trappers and settlers. The Cape Disappointment Lighthouse was built in 1856, and the North Head Lighthouse, two miles away, in 1896. They stand in one of the windiest areas of the United States. In 1921, winds at North Head were clocked at 132 miles per hour before the instruments were blown away.

Grocery stores in San Francisco's Chinatown displayed a wide array of fresh and dried foods, and herbs sold for medicinal purposes. After an earthquake and fire destroyed Chinatown and much of San Francisco in 1906, the close-knit Chinese American community decided to rebuild Chinatown with an eye to tourism.

The figures in this scene are based on photographs by Arnold Genthe. The man with a tray on his head is delivering hot food from a restaurant to a private home.

Adèle, Simon, and Aunt Cécile are riding in the area northwest of Denver, Colorado, that became Rocky Mountain National Park in 1915. Hiding in the picture are a bear, an elk, a coyote, a porcupine, a bighorn sheep, a marmot, a chipmunk, a bobcat, a bald eagle, a lizard, a rabbit, a magpie, and a mouse.

The plaza and Saint Francis Cathedral are well-known landmarks in Santa Fe, New Mexico; standing in conversation are the potter Maria Martinez, her husband, Julian, and anthropologist/archaeologist Edgar Lee Hewitt.

A typical scene of cowboys around a chuck wagon after a day of work. The poses of cowboys in the drawing are based on the prints of Texas photographer Erwin E. Smith. Smith's work from the early 1900s has preserved a record of open-range cowboy life in the Southwest.

Known as Madame John's Legacy, after a story by New Orleans author George Washington Cable, this raised cottage is thought to be the oldest building of its kind in the Mississippi Valley. It was built around 1726, damaged by fire, and rebuilt in 1788. Today, New Orleans is slowly rebuilding after the devastation caused by Hurricane Katrina in August of 2005.

The first steamboat arrived in St. Louis, Missouri, on August 2, 1817. It was a small vessel with a little engine, and the crew often had to use poles to help move it along. By the 1830s, more powerful steamboats carried cargo and passengers up and down the Mississippi and Missouri rivers. By 1908, however, train lines extended all along these rivers, and the steamboat era was fading away. Among the passengers boarding with Adèle, Simon, and Aunt Cécile are Joseph Pulitzer, Samuel Clemens (aka Mark Twain), Scott Joplin, Marianne Moore, T. S. Eliot, and a young Al Hirschfeld.

The United States Capitol in Washington, D.C., is located at the east end of the National Mall. The original design was created by a self-taught architect trained as a physician, Dr. William Thornton, and inspired by the Louvre in Paris and the Pantheon in Rome. George Washington laid the cornerstone on September 18, 1793, when building began. The majority of the workforce were African Americans, both free and enslaved. The Capitol has housed the meeting chambers of the Senate and the House of Representatives for more than two centuries.

Looking on as Simon tucks in his shirt are President Theodore "Teddy" Roosevelt, his wife Edith, and their children Alice, Ted Jr., Kermit, Ethel, Archie, and Quentin, as well as their pets—Eli Yale the macaw, Tom Quartz the cat, Sailor Boy the dog, Maude the pig, Jonathan Edwards the bear cub, Josiah the badger, Jonathan the rat, Algonquin the pony, Emily Spinach the snake, and a one-legged rooster.

To David, Mark, and Larson,
and to the people of New Orleans
—B.M.

The endpaper railway map of the United States is from the Library of Congress, Geography and Map Division.

Copyright © 2008 by Barbara McClintock
All rights reserved
Distributed in Canada by Douglas & McIntyre Ltd.
Color separations by Chroma Graphics PTE Ltd.
Printed in the United States of America by Worzalla
Designed by Irene Metaxatos
First edition, 2008
1 3 5 7 9 10 8 6 4 2

www.fsgkidsbooks.com

Library of Congress Cataloging-in-Publication Data
McClintock, Barbara.
   Adèle & Simon in America / Barbara McClintock.— 1st ed.
      p. cm.
   Summary: When Adèle and Simon visit their Aunt Cécile in New York City, she takes them on a train trip around the United States, but from Boston to San Francisco to Washington, D.C., Simon keeps losing his belongings, despite his sister's reminders. Includes facts about the places they visit.
   ISBN-13: 978-0-374-39924-5
   ISBN-10: 0-374-39924-7
   [1. Voyages and travels—Fiction.  2. Lost and found possessions—Fiction.  3. Brothers and sisters—Fiction.  4. Aunts—Fiction.]
   I. Title.  II. Title: Adèle and Simon in America.

PZ7.M47841418Adi 2008
[E]—dc22

2007016587

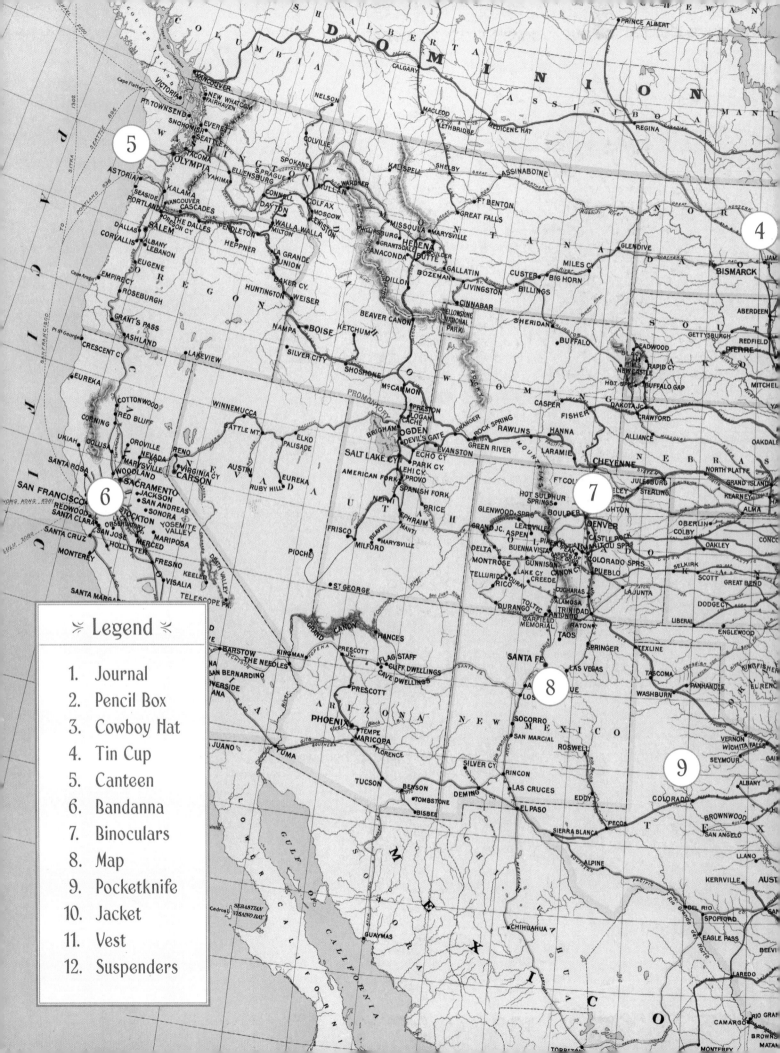

## ≽ Legend ≼

1. Journal
2. Pencil Box
3. Cowboy Hat
4. Tin Cup
5. Canteen
6. Bandanna
7. Binoculars
8. Map
9. Pocketknife
10. Jacket
11. Vest
12. Suspenders